Master of All Masters

Master of All Masters

AN ENGLISH FOLKTALE

Illustrated by Marcia Sewall

An Atlantic Monthly Press Book
Little, Brown and Company
BOSTON   TORONTO

ILLUSTRATIONS COPYRIGHT © 1972 BY MARCIA SEWALL

LIBRARY OF CONGRESS CATALOG CARD NO. 72–76290
FIRST EDITION

T 10/72

ATLANTIC-LITTLE, BROWN BOOKS
ARE PUBLISHED BY
LITTLE, BROWN AND COMPANY
IN ASSOCIATION WITH
THE ATLANTIC MONTHLY PRESS

Published simultaneously in Canada
by Little, Brown & Company (Canada) Limited

PRINTED IN THE UNITED STATES OF AMERICA

To My Mother and Father

A girl once went to the fair to hire herself out as a servant.

At last a funny-looking old gentleman engaged her,

and took her home to his house.

When she got there, he told her that he had something to teach her. In his house he had his own names for things.

He said to her, "What will you call me?"

"Master or mister, or whatever you please, sir," said she.

He said, "You must call me 'master of all masters.'"

"And what would you call this?" he said, pointing to his bed.

"Bed or couch, or whatever you please, sir."

"No, that's my 'barnacle.'"

"And what do you call these?" said he, pointing to his pantaloons.

"Breeches or trousers, or whatever you please, sir."

"You must call them 'squibs and crackers.'"

16

"And what would you call her?" he said, pointing to the cat.

"Cat or kit, or whatever you please, sir."

"You must call her 'white-faced simminy.'"

"And this now," he said, showing her the fire. "What would you call this?"

"Fire or flame, or whatever you please, sir."

"You must call it 'hot cockalorum.'"

"And what is this?" he went on, pointing to the water.

"Water or wet, or whatever you please, sir."

"No, 'pondalorum' is its name."

"And what do you call this?" asked he, as he pointed to the house.

"House or cottage, or whatever you please, sir."

"You must call it 'high topper mountain.'"

That very night the servant woke her master up in a fright and said, "Master of all masters, get out of your barnacle and put on your squibs and crackers. White-faced simminy has got a spark of hot cockalorum on her tail, and unless you get some pondalorum, high topper mountain will be all on hot cockalorum!"

And that's all.

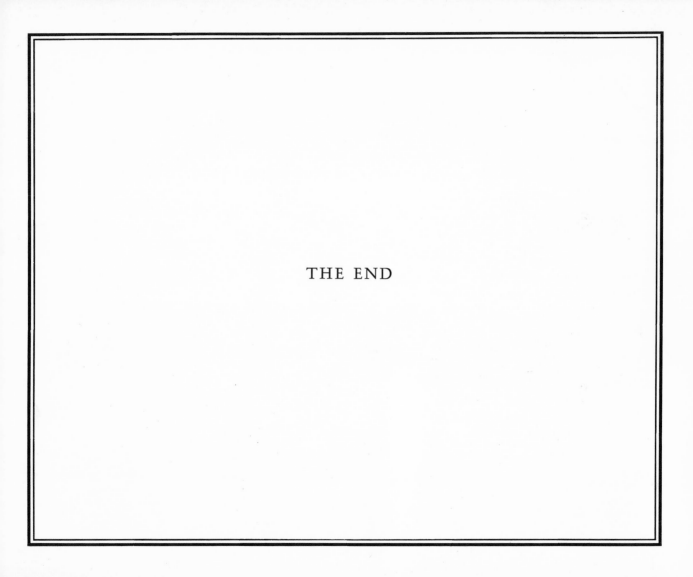

THE END